Katie Woo

Katie Saves the Earth

by Fran Manushkin

illustrated by Tammie Lyon

Katie Woo is published by Picture Window Books,
1710 Roe Crest Drive
North Mankato, Minnesota 56003
www.capstonepub.com

Text © 2013 Fran Manushkin
Illustrations © 2013 Picture Window Books

Library of Congress Cataloging-in-Publication Data
Manushkin, Fran.
  Katie saves the Earth / by Fran Manushkin; illustrated by Tammie Lyon.
      p. cm. — (Katie Woo)
  Summary: With Earth Day coming up, Katie decides to have a yard sale with her friends and recycle her old toys.
  ISBN 978-1-4048-7652-1 (library binding)
  ISBN 978-1-4048-8046-7 (pbk.)
  1. Woo, Katie (Fictitious character)—Juvenile fiction. 2. Chinese Americans—Juvenile fiction. 3. Earth Day—Juvenile fiction. 4. Garage sales—Juvenile fiction. 5. Friendship—Juvenile fiction. [1. Chinese Americans—Fiction. 2. Earth Day—Fiction. 3. Garage sales—Fiction. 4. Friendship—Fiction.] I. Lyon, Tammie, ill. II. Title. III. Series: Manushkin, Fran. Katie Woo.
  PZ7.M3195Kbk 2013
  813.54—dc2   2012029149

Art Director: Kay Fraser
Graphic Designer: Kristi Carlson

Photo Credits:
Greg Holch, pg. 26
Tammie Lyon, pg. 26

Printed in the United States of America in Stevens Point, Wisconsin.
122015
009367R

Table of Contents

Chapter 1

Earth Day

"Earth Day is coming," said Miss Winkle. "How can we keep the Earth green?"

"We can paint it green," said Katie Woo. "But we will need lots of paint."

"That is not what I mean," said Miss Winkle. "I want to keep the Earth green by taking care of the plants and trees. They need clean air and water."

"I know what to do," said

JoJo. "We can fix leaks in

our sinks. Then we won't

waste water."

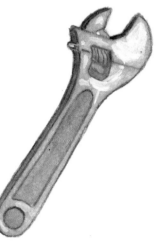

"That's a

great idea," said

Miss Winkle.

"We can reuse things," said Pedro. "My little brother sleeps in my old crib."

"I want to do something great for Earth Day," said Katie.

"I'm sure you will," said Miss Winkle.

"I know what to do!" said Katie. "I'll have a yard sale. My friends can bring things for people to reuse. That will make the Earth happy."

Chapter 2

Yard Sale Today!

On Earth Day, Katie put

her old toys on the lawn.

"Are you sure you don't

want them?" asked her mom.

"I'm sure!" said Katie.

JoJo brought a teapot without a top and a broken lamp.

"Who will want those?" wondered Katie.

Pedro brought torn jeans
and books.

"Nobody will want those
either," worried Katie.

Soon the first shopper arrived. It was Miss Winkle!

She told Pedro, "I can turn your jeans into a tote bag for my books."

Pedro's little brother Paco grabbed Katie's old elephant.

"Hey!" yelled Katie. "I put that outside by mistake."

Katie ran inside and put
the elephant back on her
bed.

Then Katie went back outside. "I hope more people come," she said.

But nobody did.

"What can we do?" Katie asked her friends.

Pedro's dad picked up
JoJo's lamp. "I can fix this
and use it at work," he said.
"Yay!" yelled JoJo.

"Pedro's books look great," said JoJo. "I can take them home to read."

"That's terrific!" yelled Pedro. "All of my stuff is gone!"

"I can put my paint brushes in JoJo's teapot," said Katie.

"Yay!" cheered JoJo. "Now all of my stuff is gone, too."

"But none of mine is gone." Katie sighed.

Chapter 3
Smart Reusing

Just then, little Paco fell

down. He cried and cried.

Katie patted him, but he

kept crying.

"Poor Paco," she said. "I

have an idea!"

Katie ran into her house.

Then she returned, holding

something behind her back.

"Surprise!" said Katie.

"Here is my elephant!"

Paco hugged it and

smiled.

"When I was little," said

Katie, "it made me feel

better, too."

"That is smart reusing,"

said Katie's mom. "But are

you sure it's okay?"

"I'm sure!" Katie smiled.

"Paco and I are both happy."

The birds were singing,

and the air smelled sweet.

"The Earth looks happy,

too," said Katie.

And it did!

About the Author

Fran Manushkin is the author of many
popular picture books, including *Baby,
Come Out!*; *Latkes and Applesauce: A
Hanukkah Story*; *The Tushy Book*; *The Belly Book*;
and *Big Girl Panties*. There is a real Katie Woo — she's Fran's
great-niece — but she never gets in half the trouble of the
Katie Woo in the books. Fran writes on her beloved Mac
computer in New York City, without the help of her
two naughty cats, Chaim and Goldy.

About the Illustrator

Tammie Lyon began her love for drawing
at a young age while sitting at the kitchen
table with her dad. She continued her love
of art and eventually attended the Columbus College of
Art and Design, where she earned a bachelors degree in fine
art. After a brief career as a professional ballet dancer, she
decided to devote herself full time to illustration. Today she
lives with her husband, Lee, in Cincinnati, Ohio. Her dogs, Gus
and Dudley, keep her company as she works in her studio.

Glossary

brought (BRAWT)—took something with you

cheered (CHIHRD)—shouted encouragement or approval

reuse (ree-YOOZ)—to use something again, especially in a new or different way

sighed (SYED)—breathed out deeply, often to express sadness or relief

terrific (tuh-RIK-ik)—very good or excellent; wonderful

Discussion Questions

1. Why is it important to take care of the Earth?

2. Did you like Katie's idea of having a yard sale on Earth Day? Why or why not?

3. Katie didn't want to give her elephant away, but she did to make Paco feel better. Have you ever done something you didn't want to because you knew it would make someone else happy?

Writing Prompts

1. List three things you can do to help save the Earth.

2. Make an Earth Day poster. Be sure to write a special message.

3. Katie talked about painting the Earth green. Write a silly story about trying to cover the Earth with paint.

Reuse Your Crayons!

Did you ever notice that after you use your crayons for a while, you end up with all sorts of short pieces? With this project, you can take all those bits and make something really cool! Just be sure to get help from a grown-up.

What you need:

- crayon pieces, no longer than an inch

- a heart-shaped muffin tin (you could use round too)

- cookie sheet

- scrap paper

What you do:

1. Ask a grown-up to heat the oven to 250 degrees.

2. Fill each muffin mold with crayon pieces. Use lots of different colors so they can swirl together.

3. Place the muffin tin in the oven. Place the cookie sheet on the rack under the tin to catch any drips. Bake until the crayons are melted, about 10 to 15 minutes.

4. Let cool. Then remove the hearts from the pan and smooth out any rough spots by rubbing them on the scrap paper.

Use your special crayons to make extra-colorful pictures. And don't forget to share some with your friends!

THE FUN DOESN'T STOP HERE!

Discover more at www.capstonekids.com

- ♥ Videos & Contests
- ✿ Games & Puzzles
- ♥ Friends & Favorites
- ✿ Authors & Illustrators

Find cool websites and more books like this one at www.facthound.com. Just type in the Book ID: **9781404876521** and you're ready to go!